JUNGA
the Dancing Yeti

by Stephen Tako illustrated by Peter Gullerud

Executive Producers

Kronenberger CPA & Company, Inc,

Don Goettling & Gino Fronti, The Don & Gino Radio Show,

Stacey Havener & Basecamp Café & Info Lounge

Associate Producers

Earhart & Associates Inc, the Kemper Family, Susan & Jeff Carpenter,

William Burton, the Strickland Family, Fred Ross, Mary Norris,

Alex Doenut Bleecker, Krysta Wallrauch, Thomas E. Rice

Junga, the Dancing Yeti
is dedicated to the following friends:
Shelby, Kelsy & Bailey Kemper
McKenzie Ross
Liam & Henry Norris
Nevlin & Livia Hartnell
Zachary Lavoie

Junga, the Dancing Yeti
Ages 4-7 Illustration Storybook

Author and Creator Stephen Tako
Illustrator Peter Gullerud

Published by CONFIDENT LIFE ENTERPRISES

ISBN-13: 978-1-7324123-0-9

Printed in the USA
Signature Book Printing, www.sbpbooks.com

Junga Yeti lived with his family in the frozen mountains. Yetis love cold snowy weather, and his poppa said the snow helped to hide and protect them from danger. The weather was too cold during the winter months for Junga, the youngest yeti. He was always jumping around to keep warm.

Momma said he was her little dancing yeti. But Brother and Sissy did not like all the moves he would make.

"Momma!" yelled Brother "He's doing it again!"

"Yeah, please tell him to stop!" cried Sissy. "Junga, can't you be normal like the rest of us?"

"Hush you two," replied Momma. "Junga, I like what you're doing."

"I-i-i-jump around, b-b-because it's t-t-too cold here and th-th-this warms me

Grandma Yeti asked Momma and Poppa if she could take Junga to a place that wasn't too cold for the winter. Junga's parents knew he would be in good hands with Grandma. They would miss their youngest yeti, but agreed this would be best for Junga.

Grandma and Junga climbed onto a ship to find a new home for the winter. The little yeti was excited about the trip. He'd never been off the snowy mountain before.

When Grandma knew they were south enough, she brought her grandson and their things through the ocean waters to the nearest land.

"Look, Junga! Can you see those big and powerful condor birds?" asked Grandma. "They need plenty of open mountain space, just like us."

"Yes, I do...I love you Grandma. Thank you for taking care of me," said Junga as he held tightly to her back.

"We made it Junga," said a tired Grandma. "Now let's find a place to rest a bit before heading up the mountain."

"YIPPIE!" yelled little Junga.

"Shhh….. We must be quiet," warned Grandma. "We need to get to the mountain top safely. So please whisper until we find a safe cave."

"I'm sorry, Grandma," whispered Junga.

Grandma noticed the air getting a little cooler and saw more pine trees. This let her know she was on the right path.

"Are we almost there, Grandma?" asked a tired Junga.

"Yes, little yeti. I believe this is a good mountain," said Grandma.

"Will we find friends here like us?" asked Junga.

"We will find friends. But not like us, Junga. Not like us," answered Grandma softly.

"Grandma, is this cave good enough for us?" asked Junga.

"No Junga, we could not both fit in there. We need to find a bigger cave," replied Grandma sounding a bit annoyed.

"HELLO IN THERE!" Junga yelled into the cave.

"Junga, please. No loud noises until I know we have found a safe place to stay," scolded Grandma.

"What do we have here?" yelled General Condor, leader of an army of huge condor birds. "A couple of beasts trying to ruin the king's festival?"

"I'm sorry," said a frightened Grandma as she moved to protect Junga. "We mean no harm… You see, we were…..."

SILENCE, YETI BEAST!! Take the old one to the king's court!" ordered General Condor.

In a flash, two large condors grabbed Grandma and flew off with her, leaving a shaking and alone little yeti.

"So, yeti beasts do exist..." said the general in a booming voice, "and feel they can walk freely on our land!" he accused. "I've heard stories of your kind and you do not belong on our peaceful mountain."

"P-p-please sir," cried Junga, "W-w-we d-don't..."

"SILENCE!!" yelled the general. You may be too young to be a threat to us, but we will take you to the king's festival locked in a cage."

"The king may reward us for this prize, but make sure the old beast is well hidden," the general said to the guards.

Poor Junga was so scared and cold in the cage. He was shaking while the condor guards teased him.

"Hey look at the little snow beast! Ooh, he's so scary! HAHAHAHA!" laughed one of the guard birds. "We've got us a monster? HAHAHA, some monster he is," teased another. "Hey! Show us a scary face! Can't you howl, baby yeti?"

Junga had no idea what they were talking about. He wished Grandma was there to help him.

"I'm sorry Grandma," Junga whispered to himself. "If it wasn't for me, we would be safe... back at home."

Junga was cold, so he shook and jumped around to warm up a bit.

"Look! He is doing his monster dance!" yelled a condor. "Oooohhhh, I'm scared of that!" laughed another guard. "HAHA, hey, what do you know? It's a dancing yeti!" howled another.

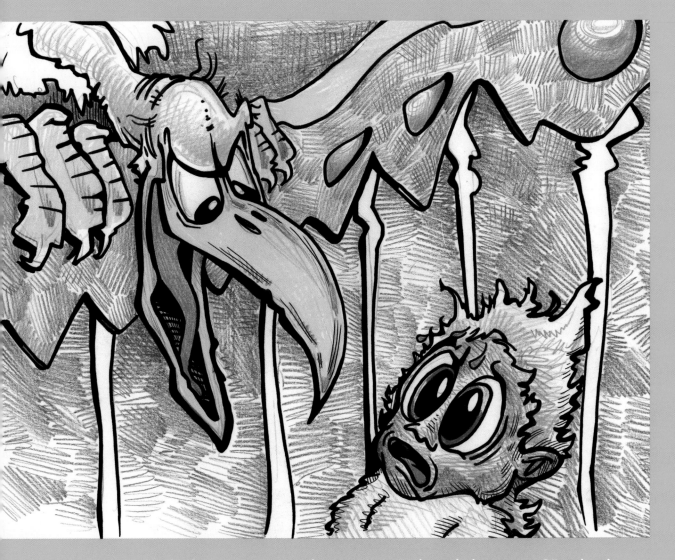

At that moment, the little yeti stopped moving. "What did you say?" asked Junga.

"I said you're a dancing yeti! HAHAHA!" laughed the condor.

"That's... that's what Momma calls me," said Junga as he burst into tears.

"Gee, little guy, you don't act like a monster. You seem like a nice little yeti," said a guard. "Why did you and the old yeti want to ruin our festival?"

"My grandma and I just got here today. We don't want to ruin anything and we're not monsters. We just wanted to find a safe cave to live in. And now... I don't know where Grandma is...." Little Junga burst into tears again.

'Aw gee, kid. What's your name?" asked one of the condor guards.

'I'm Junga," answered the brave little yeti.

Junga told them how he and his grandma left their home in search of a place that wasn't so cold for the winter.

General Condor was called over to Junga's cage.

"We hear you're a great dancer little yeti. Will you dance for us now?" asked the general. But Junga was too afraid when he saw the big condor again.

"Go on Dancing Yeti," whispered one of the guards. "This is your chance to help your grandma."

While Junga danced, the guards told the general what Junga had shared with them and that he and Grandma were not a threat.

"Perhaps our king will be happy to have a dancing yeti perform at the festival," said General Condor.

All the forest animals loved watching Junga's special dance. The king and queen condor were amazed to see how kind and lovable yetis can be once you get to know them.

Junga jumped, shook and danced his best moves to the festival music. He was performing for the royal court, but in his heart, he was dancing for Grandma. He really wished he could see her.

"GRANDMA!!" squealed a very happy little Junga. "You're OK! Oh Grandma, I missed you so much!"

"You did it, Junga!" said a delighted Grandma. "Your dancing warmed the hearts of the condors. They were scared of yetis, because we look very different from them. But they said they are really sorry and brought me here to see you right away. Plus, they have a surprise for us. Oh Junga! I'm so proud of my little dancing yeti."

The king and queen showed the yetis a wonderful cave.

"Junga," said the king. "This will be a safe winter home for you and your grandma. Can we count on you both to watch over this area for us?"

Grandma and Junga looked at each other with surprise.

"Soon," continued the king, "we condors will move down the mountain and the bears will hibernate. Yetis will be in charge of this land until next spring. Well, only if you agree."

"It would be an honor," beamed Grandma and Junga together.

"Junga?" asked Grandma. "Are you cold?"

"No Grandma," said the bouncing yeti. "I'm dancing now because I'm so happy. We have a great cave here for the winter and we've found new friends. And I'm sure we will have wonderful stories to tell everyone back home when we return next spring!"

The condors and Grandma laughed as they watched the delighted dancing yeti.

Helpful tips from Grandma Yeti

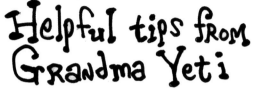

- When someone looks different from us, it's good to learn more about them.

- Be happy with yourself. Nobody else will ever be just like you.

- When someone bullies other kids, it's usually a sign that they are really sad.

- Be a friend to new children that you meet. Invite them to sit with you or to play a game.

- There is safety in numbers.

Junga's Creed

BE A LEADER...

...AND DO WHAT'S RIGHT

About the Author

As an anti-bullying advocate, Stephen Tako has interviewed children and adults wh[o] were victims of bullying on his talk show "Tako Talk". He has interviewed therapists, sports celebrities and even former bullies, to find ways to help people overcome the negative impact of being bullied. This led to his desire to reach out to children to help them fight the current epidemic of bullying.

"The strong desire to help save children from the feelings of being lost and alone has grown tremendously within me and I developed Junga to teach children about courage, acceptance and love. I too was a target of bullies and wrote about it in my book "Motivated to Act" (pub. Enchanted Forest Press 2012) in the chapter "A Damaged Child," said Tako, who is a member of the Society of Children's Book Writers and Illustrators.

Children in the USA, Ireland and Scotland have enjoyed Stephen's live readings of ho[w] Junga overcame the discrimination he and his grandmother received in the first of the Junga book series. The second book introduces Heidi, a human girl who becomes Junga[s] close friend and together they find a way to end being targets of a local bully.

Stephen Tako was born in Medina, Ohio and moved to Los Angeles at age 21. He worked mostly in the mortgage industry and the entertainment field as an actor, host, model and writer. He dedicates this book to his fiancé Marzena, his son Alex and his recently departed father, Joseph, who is depicted in this book as the late Grandpa Yeti.

About the Illustrator

Peter Gullerud is a self taught artist who presents a captivating and unique perspective in his works. His varied subject matter includes surreal landscapes, unique buildings, animated figures and tenderly portrayed wildlife. Many of his works have a mysterious story telling quality about them which allows the viewer to go on a personal imaginary journey. He uses oils and acrylics in his canvas paintings as well as a unique mixture of media in his drawings. His works suggest an unusual mix of elements reminiscent of Edvard Munch, van Gogh, Maynard Dixon, and Roger Dean along with his own unique surreal and expressive brush strokes.

Peter's expressive detail and technical gifts have been employed at the three top animation studios in Los Angeles: Hanna-Barbera, Disney Features and Warner Brothers Features. He rose up the chain at Disney becoming one of two prestigious visual development artists on the hit film Aladdin. After that, he remained a visual development artist on the Warner Brothers films Space Jam, Quest for Camelot and The Iron Giant.

After 15 years of studio work, Gullerud began working directly with wildlife. He brings to his work the authenticity of working with Wildlife Educators and Tippi Hedren's animals at the Shambala Preserve. He has hands on experiences with Siberian tigers, California black bears, binturongs, pigtail macaques, African elephants, wolves and many other exotics. After Peter's wildlife period, he began painting surrealist landscapes and continues to do that to this day. His paintings display a boundless imagination and storytelling ability that draws you into his works. As you are drawn in, you often discover surprising, hidden details within the picture that make a statement about our humanity, our planet and and the other beings we share it with. Some of the other creatures are totally original and reside solely within the surreal world of Peter's imagination.

In addition to his paintings, Peter is an accomplished illustrator creating many imaginative and whimsical drawings in his own unique fashion using ink, pencil and other media.

Peter Gullerud was born in Wisconsin and moved to California where he has spent most of his life. He resided in the quaint village of Pine Mountain Club, CA in the Los Padres National Forest where he was introduced to author Stephen Tako and began collaborating on Junga, the Dancing Yeti. He lived there for many years where his works were displayed in local businesses and sold throughout the country. Peter now resides in Taft, CA, another quaint town. Peter displays a concern for environmental issues and a compassion for all animals as evidenced in his works. He remains a member of the Animators Guild of America.